WHERE'S SANTA'S
REINDEER?

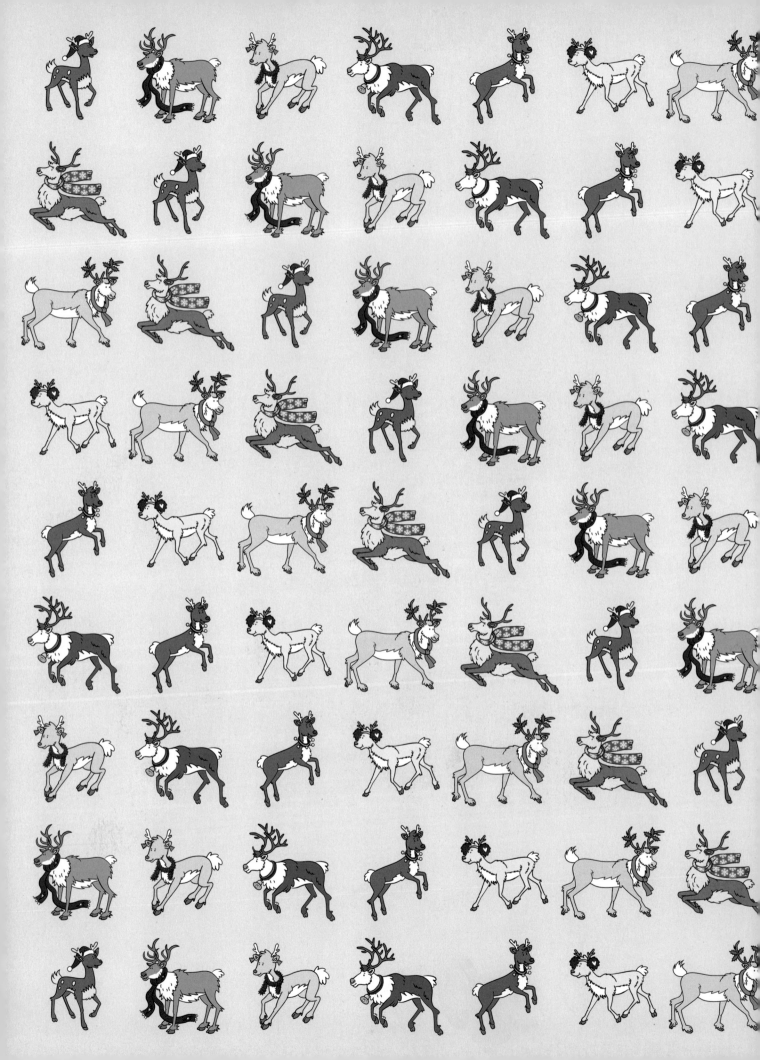

WHERE'S SANTA'S
REINDEER?

ILLUSTRATED BY
PAUL MORAN

Michael O'Mara Books Limited

INTRODUCTION

There's a week to go before Christmas Eve. Santa and his head elf, Jingle, are making some final preparations ahead of the big night when disaster strikes. Jingle has gone to check on the reindeer herd only to find that Santa's eight most-trusted reindeer are nowhere in sight!

There's nothing reindeer love more than Christmas, but Santa's team are normally too busy to celebrate. This year, Dasher and his friends are determined to take part in the festivities and have snuck off on a 'quick trip' around the world. Jingle is beside himself! The reindeer need to be in tip-top condition for Christmas Eve, and he and Santa haven't got a hope of delivering all the gifts in one night without them. They have no choice but to set off in hot pursuit.

Can you spot all eight reindeer in each festive scene, plus Santa and Jingle? The reindeer are doing their best to blend in, so you'll need to keep your eyes peeled. You can find the answers, as well as extra things to spot, at the back of the book.

DASHER

Dasher might be Santa's fastest reindeer but he wants to take his time this year to get into the Christmas spirit. He'd particularly like to visit a magical lantern display in Argentina.

DANCER

True to her name, Dancer loves rockin' around the Christmas tree. She's looking forward to doing some festive carolling and can't wait to crash a few Christmas parties.

PRANCER

Gentle Prancer loves getting into the holiday mood by making gingerbread reindeer. She's keen to visit a German Christmas market so she can pick up a new festive scarf.

COMET

Comet is obsessed with a pop group called The Reindeers. She's hoping the herd have time to catch their Christmas concert – that would be the best present EVER!

VIXEN

Vixen isn't one for sitting in front of the TV all Christmas. She loves being out and about. Top of her Christmas list is a pair of hoof-shaped roller skates – she is desperate to take part in a 'Santa Skate'.

CUPID

Cupid is dreaming of a white Christmas – even though she lives in the North Pole, she can't get enough of snow. She'll happily spend all day sledging and making her own snow reindeer.

DONNER

Donner can't think of anything more Christmassy than putting his hooves up by a roaring fire with a mulled apple juice and his favourite seasonal story – Charles Dickens' *A Christmas Carol*.

BLITZEN

Unusually for a reindeer, Blitzen's a bit of a grumpy Grinch when it comes to Christmas. The rest of the herd hope that a trip to a pantomime will melt his frosty heart.

SANTA

All this cheery fellow wants to do is deliver his presents before Christmas morning. When the job's done, he's looking forward to relaxing with a nice cup of tea and a mince pie.

JINGLE

Jingle knows they're the best flying reindeer around, but Dasher and his friends don't half make life difficult. Trust the reindeer to run off a week before the biggest night of the year …

CHRISTMAS MARKET

First stop on the herd's festive bucket list is a trip to a Christmas market in Germany. The square is packed with people browsing the stalls for stocking fillers, and the air is filled with the smell of cinnamon biscuits and the sound of a Bavarian folk band.

Dasher makes a beeline for the ice rink, while Prancer and Dancer go in search of some traditional *lebkuchen* cookies. Santa and Jingle haven't got a hope of rounding up the reindeer in this crowd, so they decide to grab a hot chocolate and soak up the atmosphere, too.

Can you spot the eight reindeer, Santa and Jingle?

SHOPPING MALL

The reindeer have heard that people often visit shopping malls in the run-up to Christmas, so they've decided to pay one a visit to see what the fuss is about. The herd are rather taken with the sparkly decorations and window displays, but they don't understand why people are buying so many presents – can't they just wait a few days for Santa's delivery?

All the reindeer are intrigued by the 'Santa's Grotto' and Cupid wants to have a go on the escalator. Dancer is disappointed to find that none of the shops sell clothing suitable for her (despite the reindeer in the window).

Can you spot the eight reindeer, Santa and Jingle?

CHRISTMAS LANTERNS

The herd have whizzed down to Argentina so they can take part in a magical festive tradition. Every year, families and friends come together at Christmas to release hundreds of paper lanterns, or *globos*, into the sky. It's an incredible sight.

The reindeer head into the crowd to join in the celebrations. Blitzen wants to light a lantern himself and Dasher is keen to try some homemade *pan dulce* – a sweet, fruity bread – from the food stand.

Can you spot the eight reindeer, Santa and Jingle?

TREE FARM

Next stop is a Christmas tree farm in Sweden. Families have come from miles around to pick their perfect tree, as well as stock up on some handmade decorations and goodies from the farm shop.

After the long flight from Argentina, the sight and scent of all these trees is making the reindeer a little peckish – Vixen can't resist having a nibble of a particularly succulent-looking fir. Santa and Jingle better be quick, or the reindeer are in danger of eating up the whole farm.

Can you spot the eight reindeer, Santa and Jingle?

TRAIN STATION

To save their strength for flying, the reindeer have decided to treat themselves to a relaxing train ride to their next destination. But they hadn't banked on the holiday crowds. The station is full of people trying to beat the Christmas rush, so Dancer runs on ahead to grab the herd some seats.

Despite the mayhem, the rest of the reindeer are enjoying the cheery brass band and Donner is enchanted by the retro 'Santa Express'. There's no time to dawdle, though, if they want to give Santa and Jingle the slip and catch that train.

Can you spot the eight reindeer, Santa and Jingle?

1920s PARTY

The reindeer can't remember the last time Santa threw a Christmas party at the North Pole – the week before Christmas is so busy, there's not usually time – so they are over the moon to be the guests of honour at this exclusive 1920s-themed do.

Dancer is discovering her inner flapper girl and trying to master a complicated dance called the lindy hop. Even Santa's getting into the swing of things. Poor Jingle has tried in vain to keep the herd under control and found himself caught up in a show dance instead.

Can you spot the eight reindeer, Santa and Jingle?

LET IT SNOW

Cupid has heard that the place to be in New York at Christmas is Central Park, so she's persuaded the herd to join her there for an afternoon. It's packed with families enjoying the crisp snow and winter sunshine.

Cupid is in her element and heads straight up the slope to see if someone will let her have a go on their sledge. Vixen has wasted no time in joining a snowball fight, while Dasher wants to lend a hoof and help a group of friends build a snowman.

Can you spot the eight reindeer, Santa and Jingle?

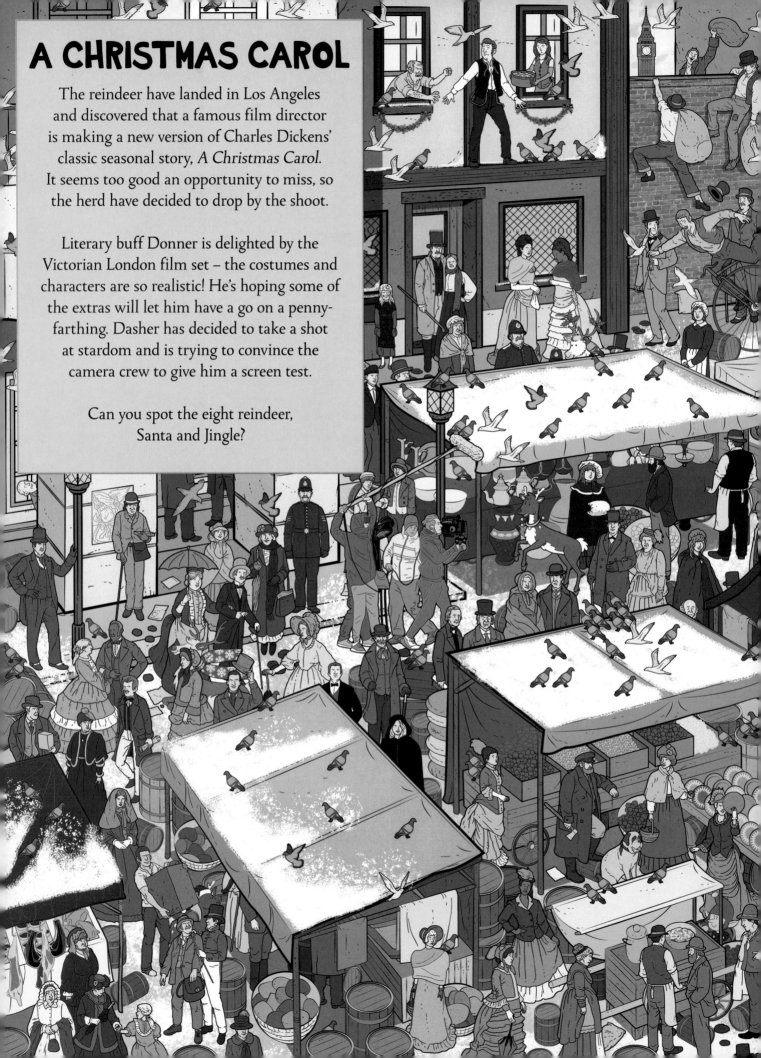

A CHRISTMAS CAROL

The reindeer have landed in Los Angeles and discovered that a famous film director is making a new version of Charles Dickens' classic seasonal story, *A Christmas Carol*. It seems too good an opportunity to miss, so the herd have decided to drop by the shoot.

Literary buff Donner is delighted by the Victorian London film set – the costumes and characters are so realistic! He's hoping some of the extras will let him have a go on a penny-farthing. Dasher has decided to take a shot at stardom and is trying to convince the camera crew to give him a screen test.

Can you spot the eight reindeer, Santa and Jingle?

SYDNEY

The herd have arrived down under. Huge crowds have assembled outside the world-famous opera house to catch a special Christmas concert, and the reindeer are just in time to get some last-minute tickets.

While the reindeer wait for the doors to open, Dancer joins a group of carol singers to belt out 'We Wish You a Merry Christmas' and Comet admires the views across the harbour. Santa is finding it a bit hot in his woolly suit and hat, and is toying with the idea of taking part in a 'Santa Surf' to cool down.

Can you spot the eight reindeer, Santa and Jingle?

SANTA SKATE

Vixen is super excited to be taking part in her first 'Santa Skate'. Hundreds of people have strapped on their roller skates and dressed up in festive costumes to celebrate the start of the holiday season.

This city centre is full of party-goers and tourists, and Vixen wastes no time in setting off to find some reindeer-shaped skates so she can join in the fun. Meanwhile, Blitzen's got caught up in the crowd and is causing chaos. Donner and Prancer have decided it's much safer to watch the action from the sides.

Can you spot the eight reindeer, Santa and Jingle?

ICE PARK

The reindeer are visiting an ice park in China that's hosting an incredible display of frozen sculptures. People have come from far and wide to admire the delicate statues and watch the sculptors at work.

The herd are having fun exploring the twinkly ice palace and making friends with the park's cute penguins. Prancer has headed straight for the ice slide, while Dasher is impressed with the (he thinks rather handsome) reindeer statues. He wonders if he can persuade Santa to take one home to the North Pole.

Can you spot the eight reindeer, Santa and Jingle?

POST OFFICE

The reindeer are used to letters arriving by chimney, so a stop off at this busy post office in Rome is a bit of an eye-opener. The place is jam-packed with people trying to catch the last Christmas post. It's even more hectic than Santa's workshop!

The reindeer are intrigued by all the goings-on. Donner is keen to take home some seasonal stamps as a souvenir, but he's having trouble operating the self-service machine with his hooves. Jingle, meanwhile, can't help but offer stressed-out customers advice on the best way to wrap a present.

Can you spot the eight reindeer, Santa and Jingle?

ROCKIN' REINDEER

Comet cannot *believe* the reindeer have managed to score tickets to a Christmas performance by her number-one favourite band – The Reindeers!

While Comet is busy shouting out requests for 'All the Jingle Ladies' and 'Sleigh My Name', Dancer's busting some moves near the front of the stage. It's all a bit much for poor Jingle – and he has no idea where Santa's got to – so he's gone to look for a quiet seat at the back of the arena.

Can you spot the eight reindeer, Santa and Jingle?

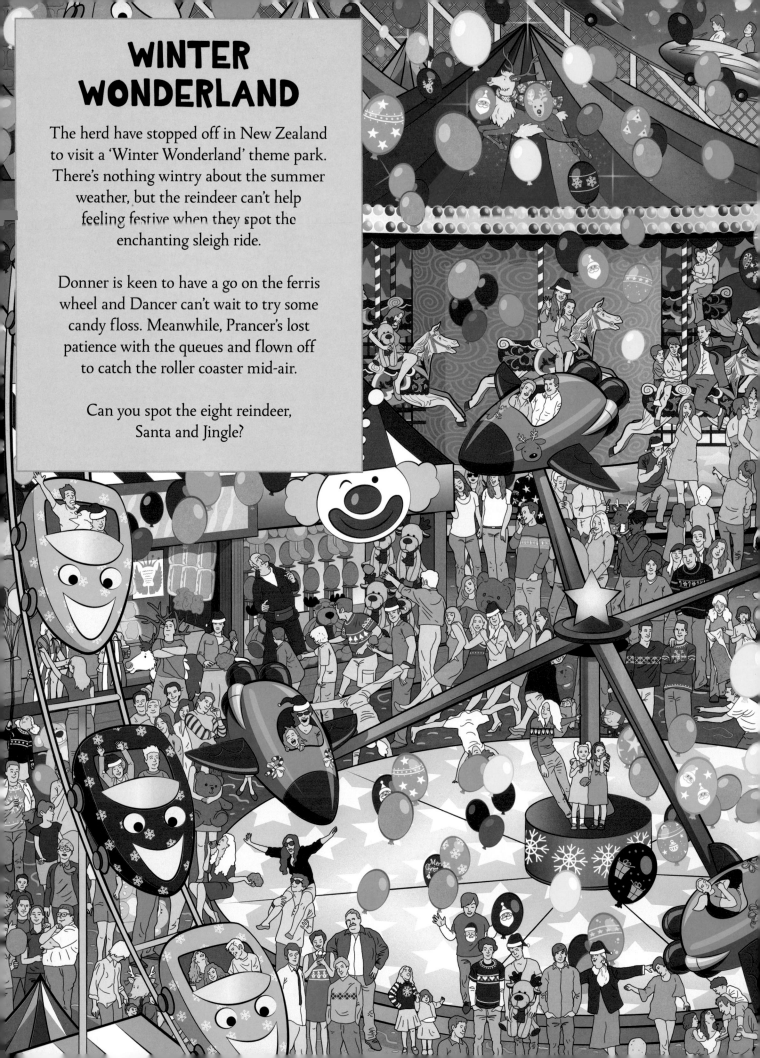

WINTER WONDERLAND

The herd have stopped off in New Zealand to visit a 'Winter Wonderland' theme park. There's nothing wintry about the summer weather, but the reindeer can't help feeling festive when they spot the enchanting sleigh ride.

Donner is keen to have a go on the ferris wheel and Dancer can't wait to try some candy floss. Meanwhile, Prancer's lost patience with the queues and flown off to catch the roller coaster mid-air.

Can you spot the eight reindeer, Santa and Jingle?

IT'S CHRISTMAS!

What's this ... another Christmas party? The reindeer can't get enough of the festivities and have decided to crash a fancy-dress extravaganza. They're impressed by all the costumes and figure they'll blend into the crowd pretty nicely.

After several non-stop days on the road, the toasty fire and hearty food are very welcome. Comet has gone to see what's on offer at the buffet and Donner is soaking up the ambience with a glass of mulled apple juice. Blitzen is finally getting into the Christmas spirit and is letting his antlers down on the dance floor.

Can you spot the eight reindeer, Santa and Jingle?

PANTOMIME

It's the night before Christmas Eve and the reindeer know they have to head home soon. There's just time to catch a performance of the classic pantomime *Cinderella* before they do.

Prancer and Blitzen want to get as close to the stage as they can, while Comet and Dasher have decided to put their hooves up in style in the boxes. Before the reindeer can shout 'He's behind you!', they spot Santa sneaking on to the stage for the curtain call. It's time to finish their ice creams and head back to the North Pole.

Can you spot the eight reindeer, Santa and Jingle?

FLYING HOME FOR CHRISTMAS

Phew! Santa, Jingle and the reindeer have returned to the North Pole in the nick of time – the rest of the herd were starting to worry.

The reindeer have loved seeing how Christmas is celebrated around the world. Even Jingle has got to admit, it was nice not to spend the whole week worrying about presents. Now to load up that sleigh, deliver those gifts and Santa and his team can all have the rest of the year off. In the words of Donner's favourite author, 'A merry Christmas to everybody!'

Can you spot the eight reindeer, Santa and Jingle?

ANSWERS

SPOTTER'S CHECKLIST

CHRISTMAS MARKET

- A child with a blue rabbit toy ☐
- A heart-shaped biscuit ☐
- A man who has lost his glasses ☐
- A runaway dog ☐
- Three bear hats ☐

SHOPPING MALL

SPOTTER'S CHECKLIST

- Two girls fighting over a present ☐
- A messy eater ☐
- An elf with a burger ☐
- A dinosaur toy ☐
- A dog in a handbag ☐

SPOTTER'S CHECKLIST

- A green picnic hamper ☐
- Four sparklers ☐
- A man eating a whole cake ☐
- Four friends taking a selfie ☐
- A green chair ☐

SPOTTER'S CHECKLIST

- A green and pink present ☐
- A child in a pushchair ☐
- A tree being cut down ☐
- A yellow and white scarf ☐
- A dog ☐

TREE FARM

TRAIN STATION

SPOTTER'S CHECKLIST

- A brass band ☐
- Some striped orange leggings ☐
- A woman knitting ☐
- A mum, son and dog running for the train ☐
- A backpack with a heart on it ☐

SPOTTER'S CHECKLIST

1920s
PARTY

A tray being knocked over ☐

A man in a red suit and
Santa hat ☐

An old-fashioned
photographer ☐

Two black fans ☐

The conductor ☐

SPOTTER'S CHECKLIST

Two dogs on sledges ☐

A baby snowman ☐

A squirrel ☐

Three little kids on a sledge ☐

A child in a red and green
snowsuit ☐

LET IT
SNOW

A
CHRISTMAS
CAROL

SPOTTER'S CHECKLIST

A chimney sweep ☐

A monkey ☐

Sherlock Holmes ☐

A brown cat ☐

Tiny Tim's crutch ☐

SYDNEY

SPOTTER'S CHECKLIST

Two surfboards ☐

A didgeridoo ☐

A woman with a red dress and red shoes ☐

A woman wearing blue antlers ☐

A bowler hat ☐

SPOTTER'S CHECKLIST

Two reindeer onesies ☐

Someone wearing green glasses ☐

A spotty dog ☐

A pink shirt with blue stars on it ☐

A pram ☐

SANTA SKATE

ICE PARK

SPOTTER'S CHECKLIST

Two reindeer statues ☐

A snowmobile ☐

A penguin on a snowboard ☐

A girl dressed as a princess ☐

A man with a Santa hat and beard (who's not Santa) ☐

POST OFFICE

SPOTTER'S CHECKLIST

Two reindeer-shaped parcels ☐

A man in a suit who is checking his watch ☐

A purple rucksack ☐

A jumper with a reindeer face on it ☐

A red and white parcel with a green bow ☐

SPOTTER'S CHECKLIST

A milkshake being spilt ☐

A box of carrots ☐

A fight over a jumper ☐

Someone in a reindeer onesie ☐

A black and purple rucksack ☐

ROCKIN' REINDEER

WINTER WONDER-LAND

SPOTTER'S CHECKLIST

A fortune teller ☐

Two children fighting over a soft toy ☐

A T-shirt with a gingerbread man on it ☐

A woman eating four ice creams ☐

Four balloons with reindeer on them ☐

IT'S
CHRISTMAS!

SPOTTER'S CHECKLIST

A candy cane costume ☐

A unicorn costume ☐

A reindeer portrait ☐

Three Yule logs ☐

A cupcake hat ☐

SPOTTER'S CHECKLIST

Eight red roses ☐

A hat with rabbit ears ☐

An ice-cream accident ☐

A boy reading a book ☐

A chef ☐

PANTOMIME

FLYING
HOME FOR
CHRISTMAS

SPOTTER'S CHECKLIST

A reindeer skiing ☐

A reindeer with green
star earrings ☐

A reindeer wearing a
Christmas wreath ☐

A baby reindeer with a
bobble hat ☐

A reindeer with a
multi-coloured scarf ☐

ADDITIONAL ARTWORK BY GERGELY FÓRIZS, JORGE SANTILLAN AND ADAM LINLEY

WRITTEN BY FRANCES EVANS

DESIGNED BY JOHN BIGWOOD AND JACK CLUCAS

Published in Great Britain in 2019 by Michael O'Mara Books Limited,
9 Lion Yard, Tremadoc Road, London SW4 7NQ

W www.mombooks.com f Michael O'Mara Books 🐦 @OMaraBooks

This book contains material previously published in *Where's The Meerkat?*,
Where's The Meerkat? On Holiday, *Where's The Meerkat? Journey Through Time*,
Where's the Zombie?, *Where's One Direction?* and *Where's the Llama?*

A CIP catalogue record for this book is available from the British Library.

ISBN: 978-1-78929-169-8

1 3 5 7 9 10 8 6 4 2

This book was printed in August 2019 by
Shenzhen Wing King Tong Paper Products Co. Ltd.,
Shenzhen, Guangdong, China.

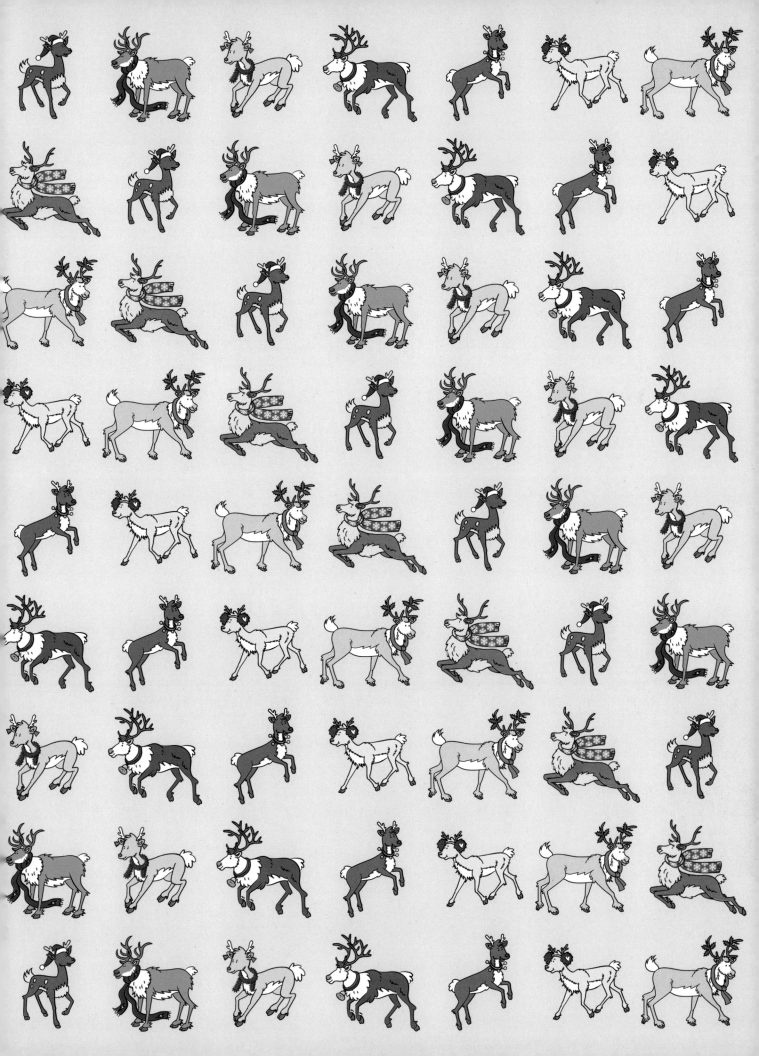